Sally's Great Balloon Adventure

Written and Illustrated by
Stephen Huneck

Abrams Books for Young Readers
New York

As a special treat, Sally's family is taking her to a balloon festival. Sally knows what a balloon is, but . . .

Sally has never seen a hot air balloon.

You can imagine her surprise when she sees
the giant balloons rising up into the air.

Sally smells some fried chicken.
She follows her nose to a balloon gondola.
The gondola is the basket the rider sits in.

As the people watch the balloons,
Sally watches the chicken.

Sally climbs the stairs to investigate
the wonderful chicken smell.

Uh-oh!
Sally falls in!

Worried, Sally grabs a rope to pull
herself out. She gives it a mighty tug.

Whoops!
Suddenly she feels lighter.

Sally hears everyone calling her name.
Their voices become quieter and quieter
until she can't hear them at all.

Sally

Sally

Sally

Sally

Sally is curious. She peeks over the edge
of the gondola. The people look like
little tiny dots far, far below.

Sally is flying in the sky like a bird!

Instead of being scared, Sally feels lucky to be alone with such delicious-smelling chicken.

Back on earth, breaking news!
The radio and newspapers all talk about
Sally aboard a runaway hot air balloon.

The TV news shows Sally's puppy pictures
and interviews people who know her.

They send helicopters to
tape Sally's air adventure.

In the gondola, Sally takes a peek inside the picnic basket. She just wants to make sure the chicken is OK.

Reports of Sally sightings start
coming in from everywhere.
Everyone wants to save Sally.

Some people's ideas for how to
save Sally seem really crazy.

Someone even suggests
sending in the air force!

Meanwhile, back in the balloon,
Sally wakes up from a wonderful nap.
She was dreaming of the fried chicken.

Her balloon drifts closer to the ground.

A child in a schoolyard recognizes Sally's balloon. Her family flies a balloon, and she knows just what to do.

She yells, "Sally, Sally! Tug-of-war, tug-of-war, Sally!" Soon all the kids are yelling, "Sally! Tug-of-war!"

Sally hears her name, and the name of her
favorite game—and so she jumps up and
gives the rope a mighty tug. Whooooooosh!

A blast of warm air escapes from the
balloon. A few moments later, Sally feels
a bump as her gondola touches down.

The children saved Sally! One of them finds the picnic basket full of chicken. The kids and their teacher take turns feeding it to Sally.

The balloon ride was fun, but Sally is glad to be back on earth with her new friends and a full tummy.

ARTIST'S NOTE

To create a woodcut print, I first draw the design of the future print in crayon, laying out the prospective shapes and colors. I then carve one block of wood for each color in the appropriate shape. The result is a series of carved blocks, one for each color in the print. After a block has been inked with its repective color, acid-free archival paper is laid onto the block and hand rubbed. I repeat the process for each color block. When this process is completed, I hang the prints to dry. —S.H.

Library of Congress Cataloging-in-Publication Data

Huneck, Stephen.
Sally's great balloon adventure / by Stephen Huneck.
p. cm.
Summary: Lured into a hot air balloon by the smell of fried chicken, Sally the black Labrador retriever inadvertently goes for a ride all by herself.
ISBN 978-0-8109-8331-1
[1. Labrador retriever—Fiction. 2. Dogs—Fiction. 3. Hot air balloons—Fiction.   I. Title.

PZ7.H8995Sb 2009
[E —dc22
2008046185

Book design by Melissa Arnst

Published in 2010 by Abrams Books for Young Readers, an imprint of ABRAMS.

Printed and bound in China
10 9 8 7 6 5 4 3 2 1

Abrams Books for Young Readers are available at special discounts when purchased in quantity for premiums and promotions as well as fundraising or educational use. Special editions can also be created to specification. For details, contact specialmarkets@abramsbooks.com or the address below.

THE ART OF BOOKS SINCE 1949
115 West 18th Street
New York, NY 10011
www.abramsbooks.com